Y0-BED-550

The Story of
Myrtle Marie

OTHER BOOKS BY CAROLYN GRAHAM
Published by Harcourt Brace & Company

THE STORY OF
THE FISHERMAN AND THE TURTLE PRINCESS

BIG CHANTS: I Went Walking

BIG CHANTS: The Napping House

THE CHOCOLATE CAKE: Songs and Poems for Children

•
_____
•

Also available:
The Story of Myrtle Marie Audio Cassette
(0-15-599733-5)

The Story of
Myrtle Marie

by Carolyn Graham
Illustrated by John Himmelman

HARCOURT
BRACE
ESL/EFL

Harcourt Brace & Company

Orlando   San Diego   New York
Toronto   London   Sydney   Tokyo

Copyright © 1995 by Harcourt Brace & Company.

All rights reserved. No part of this publication may be reproduced or transmitted in any form or by any means, electronic or mechanical, including photocopy, recording, or any information storage and retrieval system, without permission in writing from the publisher.

Requests for permission to make copies of any part of the work should be mailed to: Permissions Department, Harcourt Brace & Company, 6277 Sea Harbor Drive, Orlando, Florida 32887-6777.

Project Editor:	Marilyn Rosenthal
Production Manager:	Anne Burkett
Production:	G&H SOHO, Inc.
Cover Design:	John Himmelman
Packager:	Syntactix International

Printed in the United States of America

5 6 7 8 9 0 1 2 3 4 139 9 8 7 6 5 4 3 2 1

0-15-599702-5

The Story of Myrtle Marie

I found a turtle down by the sea.
I took that turtle dancing with me.
I named that turtle Myrtle Marie.
I loved my turtle. Myrtle loved me.

First she was happy. First she was glad.
Then she got homesick. Then she felt bad.
She missed her mother. She missed her dad.
Myrtle was lonely. Myrtle was sad.

I took my turtle back to the sea.
I said, "Goodbye, dear Myrtle Marie."
I know that somewhere down by the sea,
there is a turtle thinking of me.

ACKNOWLEGMENTS

I would like to gratefully acknowledge the creative efforts of

the artist, John Himmelman

the musician, Joseph Mennonna

and especially of

Marilyn Rosenthal

who put it all together.

DEDICATED TO
THE GRAHAM GIRLS

Libby	Robyn
Natalie	Nicole
Melissa	Ashley

I found a turtle down by the sea.

I took that turtle dancing with me.

I named that turtle Myrtle Marie.

I loved my turtle. Myrtle loved me.

First she was happy. First she was glad.

Then she got homesick. Then she felt bad.

She missed her mother. She missed her dad.

Myrtle was lonely. Myrtle was sad.

I took my turtle back to the sea.

I said, "Goodbye, dear Myrtle Marie."

I know that somewhere down by the sea,

there is a turtle thinking of me.

The Story of Myrtle Marie

I found a turtle down by the sea.
I took that turtle dancing with me.
I named that turtle Myrtle Marie.
I loved my turtle. Myrtle loved me.

First she was happy. First she was glad.
Then she got homesick. Then she felt bad.
She missed her mother. She missed her dad.
Myrtle was lonely. Myrtle was sad.

I took my turtle back to the sea.
I said, "Goodbye, dear Myrtle Marie."
I know that somewhere down by the sea,
there is a turtle thinking of me.